HOORAY FOR
Hoppy!

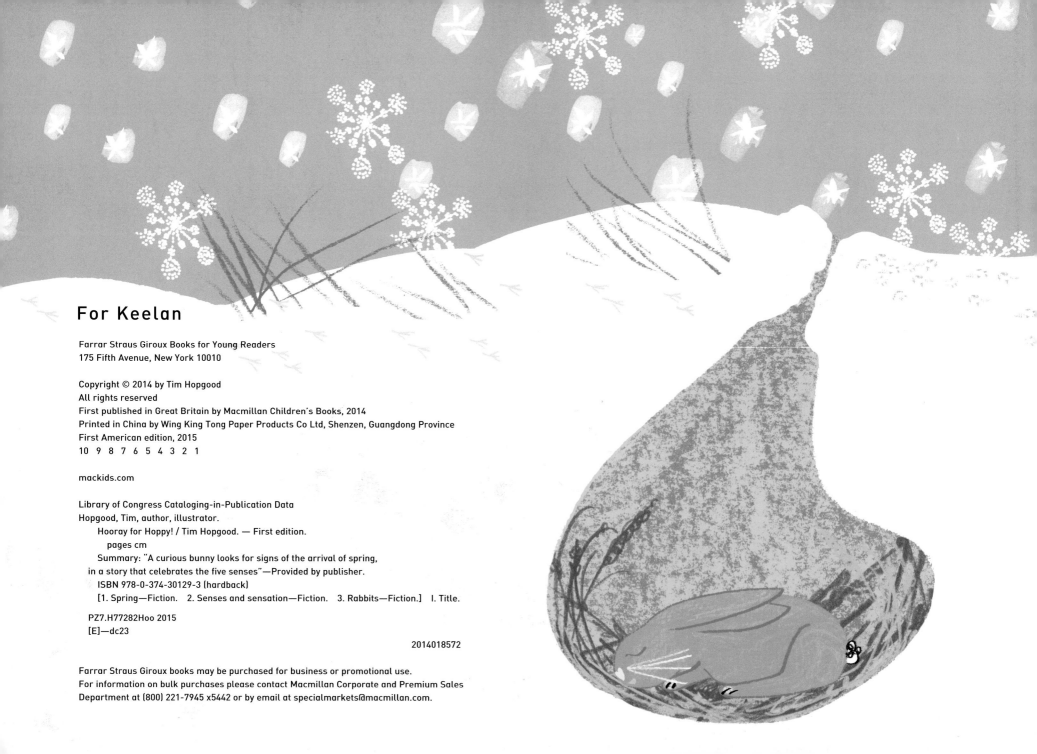

For Keelan

Farrar Straus Giroux Books for Young Readers
175 Fifth Avenue, New York 10010

First published in Great Britain by Macmillan Children's Books, 2014
Printed in China by Wing King Tong Paper Products Co Ltd, Shenzen, Guangdong Province
First American edition, 2015
10 9 8 7 6 5 4 3 2 1

mackids.com

Library of Congress Cataloging-in-Publication Data
Hopgood, Tim, author, illustrator.
    Hooray for Hoppy! / Tim Hopgood. — First edition.
        pages cm
    Summary: "A curious bunny looks for signs of the arrival of spring,
in a story that celebrates the five senses"—Provided by publisher.
    ISBN 978-0-374-30129-3 (hardback)
    [1. Spring—Fiction.   2. Senses and sensation—Fiction.   3. Rabbits—Fiction.]   I. Title.

PZ7.H77282Hoo 2015
[E]—dc23   2014018572

Farrar Straus Giroux books may be purchased for business or promotional use.
For information on bulk purchases please contact Macmillan Corporate and Premium Sales
Department at (800) 221-7945 x5442 or by email at specialmarkets@macmillan.com.

HOORAY FOR
Hoppy!

tim hopgood

Farrar Straus Giroux
New York

Hoppy woke up bright and early.

He wiggled his nose and sniffed the air.

Perhaps today's the day! he thought.

But as he hopped to the top of his

hole, he saw that the world was

covered in snow.

"Too cold," he said, and he hopped

back to bed.

The next morning, when Hoppy hopped to the top of his hole, his nose felt cold and the grass felt crunchy.

"Too icy," he said, and he hopped back to bed.

A few days later, Hoppy woke

up much earlier than usual.

Perhaps today's the day!

he thought.

Hoppy twitched his nose.

The air smelled fresh.

Perhaps today *really is* the day.

The day that spring arrives!

So Hoppy hopped down the hill

to see if it was true . . .

"Hooray!" said Hoppy, as he heard the birds singing.

"It **sounds** like spring has sprung."

"Hooray!" said Hoppy, as he sniffed the pretty flowers.

"It **smells** like spring has sprung."

"Hooray!" said Hoppy, as he watched

the lambs in the meadow.

"It **looks** like spring has sprung."

"Hooray!" said Hoppy, as he nibbled the fresh green grass.

"It **tastes** like spring has sprung."

"Hip hip hooray!" said Hoppy,

as his feet touched the warm ground.

"It even **feels** like spring has sprung."

Today really is the day! thought Hoppy.

He couldn't wait to see his friends.

But when he reached

the top of the hill . . .

. . . nobody was there!

So he thumped his back feet as hard and
as loud as he possibly could . . .

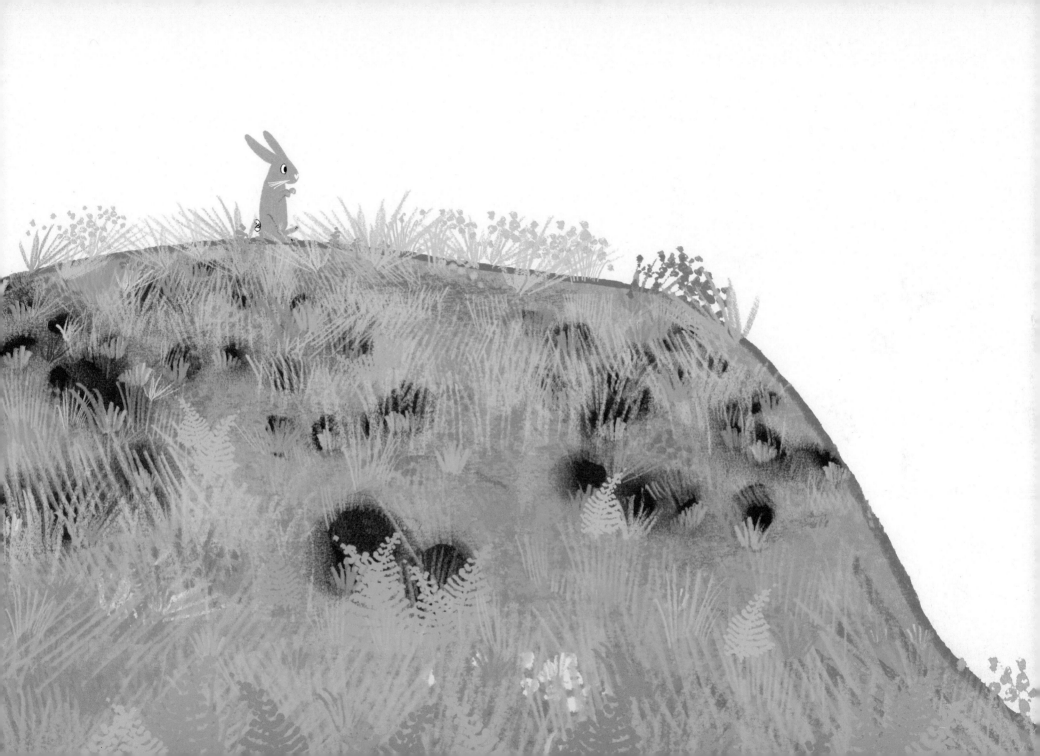

"Hooray!" shouted all the rabbits,

as Hoppy leaped high in the air.

Spring had definitely and most wonderfully sprung!

There are five senses that we use to discover the world.

1
Hearing

We listen with our ears.
What can you hear?

What does Hoppy hear?

2
Smell

We smell with our noses.
What can you smell?

What does Hoppy smell?

3
Sight

We see with our eyes.
What can you see?

What does Hoppy see?

4
Taste

We taste with our tongues.
What can you taste?

What does Hoppy taste?

5
Touch

We feel with our hands and feet.
What can you feel?

What does Hoppy feel?